Even for a Mouse

Even

for a Mouse

Story and pictures by LISL WEIL

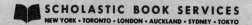
SCHOLASTIC BOOK SERVICES
NEW YORK · TORONTO · LONDON · AUCKLAND · SYDNEY · TOKYO

Copyright © 1976 by Lisl Weil. All rights reserved. Published by Scholastic Book Services, a division of Scholastic Magazines, Inc.

12 11 10 9 8 7 6 5 4 3 2   6 7 8 9/7 0 1/8

Printed in the U.S.A.

to my sister Ollie
and Maxi, Marcia and
specially to Boris ~

This is Mrs. Ollie Mouse and her darling
daughter, Little Ollie.

This is Mr. A. H. Cat.
A. H. stands for always hungry.

They live in one house.

But not together.

Every day Mrs. Mouse gives Little Ollie lessons.

An exercise lesson . . .

A cooking lesson . . .

And a foreign language lesson.

"A foreign language is most helpful in life,"
Mrs. Mouse likes to say.

Mrs. Mouse loves Little Ollie.

Mr. A. H. Cat loves Little Ollie too . . .

MENU

FRIED MOUSE CUTLETS..

MOUSE FRITTERS ..

MOUSE CHOP SUEY ..

ROAST SIRLOIN OF MOUSE ..

MOUSE STEW ..

MOUSE CHOPS PIZZICATA ..

MOUSE GIBLETS ...

. . . for his own personal reasons, of course.

One morning Mrs. Mouse had to go shopping.
"Now stay home and practice your lessons,"
she said to Little Ollie.
"Don't open the door to anyone while I'm gone."

As soon as Mrs. Mouse left the house,
Mr. Cat ran up to the door.
"Knock, knock, knock. It's the mailman," he called.
"I have a big package for you. Open the door."

"I'm busy doing my exercises," Little Ollie said.
"Come back when my mama is here."

"All right," said the cat.
But he did not really mean it.

"Knock, knock, knock."
He was at the door again.
"You have won a big prize on a TV show.
Open the door," he said, "and here it is."

"I'm busy frying corn fritters,"
Little Ollie said.
"Come back when my mama is here."

And she would not open the door.

Little Ollie opened her foreign language book.
But she did not feel like studying.
"I'll never use a foreign language anyhow,"
she thought. "Why don't I climb up that hill and
pick some flowers, instead?"

So that's what she did.

Only the hill wasn't really a hill . . .
It was Mr. Cat!
In a wink, he caught Little Ollie.

"Tralala, oh what a delight,
To have tender mouse stew
For dinner tonight," the cat sang.

Little Ollie was scared.
But she said, "You'll enjoy your dinner more
if you exercise first."

"Really?" said the cat.

"Oh, yes!" said Little Ollie.

"I'll show you some exercises my mama taught me.
First you swing your legs up and down like this.

Then bend your knees
and count to ten."

"One . . . two . . . three . . . four . . ."

Little Ollie began to run.
She ran very fast.

But not quite fast enough.

"Caught you!" sang the cat.
"I am the winner!
And now for some mouse stew.
It's almost time for dinner."

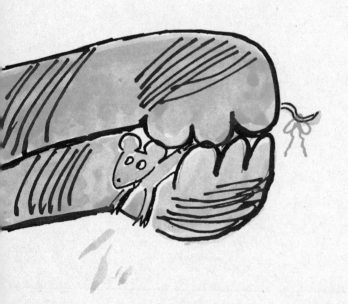

Little Ollie was more scared than ever.
But she said, "I know a way
to make your stew taste twice as nice."

"Really?" said the cat.

"Oh, yes," said Little Ollie.
"Let me show you the recipe my mama taught me.
But first we must pick some bay leaves
and mustard seeds."

Little Ollie began to run.
She ran very fast.

But not quite fast enough.

"Recipe or not,
You're going right into the pot," said the cat.
And he started for his kitchen.

"Help! Help!" cried Little Ollie.
But nobody heard her.
"Oh, my!" she thought.
"What will I do now?"

Suddenly she remembered something.
She took a deep breath and then . . .

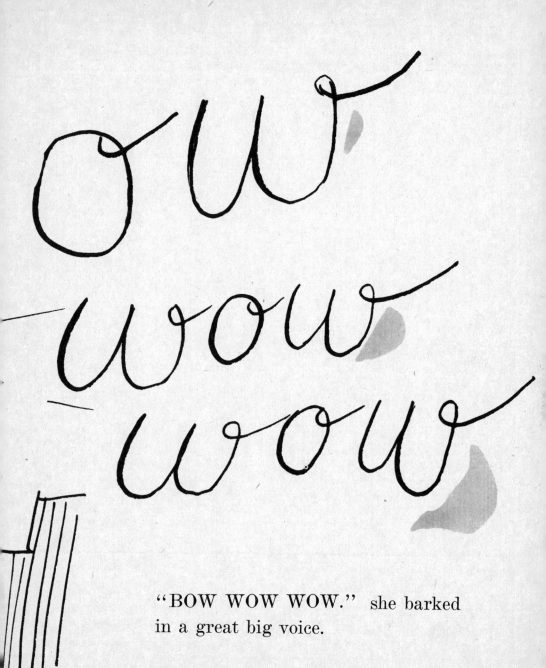

"BOW WOW WOW." she barked
in a great big voice.

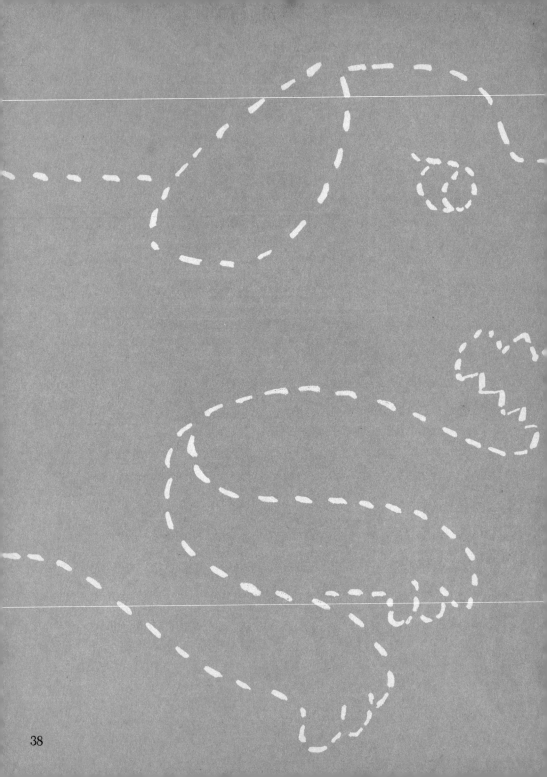

"Help! A dog!" cried Mr. Cat.

And in a jiffy he was up a tree.

Little Ollie didn't lose a second.

She ran and ran and she didn't stop
until she was safe in her house.

She was still out of breath
when Mrs. Mouse came home.

"I see you've been exercising," Mrs. Mouse said.
"Did you practice your language lesson too?"

"Yes," said Little Ollie.
"Let me show you. BOW WOW WOW."

"Very good," said her mama.
"A foreign language is most helpful in life."

"Oh, yes," said Little Ollie.
"Even for a mouse!"